OLYMPIC SPORTS/Crestwood House

5 Volumes		**Set Price $64.75/Each Title $12.95**
CWH–089686–OLYS	_____	SET
CWH–089686–6661	_____	Gymnastics/Haycock
CWH–089686–6696	_____	Skiing/Haycock
CWH–089686–670X	_____	Swimming And Diving/Sandelson
CWH–089686–6718	_____	Track Athletics/Sandelson
RPJ–075020–2319	_____	* Ice Sports

gymnastics

OLYMPIC SPORTS

kate haycock

Crestwood House
New York

Maxwell Macmillan International
New York   Oxford   Singapore   Sydney

OLYMPIC SPORTS

TRACK ATHLETICS
FIELD ATHLETICS
SWIMMING AND DIVING
GYMNASTICS
ICE SPORTS
SKIING
BALL SPORTS
COMBAT SPORTS

Designer: Ross George
Editor: Deborah Elliott

Cover photo: Mary Lou Retton of the United States performs her floor routine in front of a delighted home audience at the Games in Los Angeles in 1984.

CRESTWOOD HOUSE

Macmillan Publishing Company
866 Third Avenue
New York, NY 10022

Macmillan Publishing Company is part of the Maxwell Communication Group of Companies.

First published in Great Britain in 1991
by Wayland (Publishers) Ltd
61 Western Road, Hove, East Sussex BN3 1JD

Printed in Italy by G. Canale & C.S.p.A.
1 2 3 4 5 6 7 8 9 10

ACKNOWLEDGMENTS

The Publisher would like to thank the following agencies and photographers for allowing their pictures to be reproduced in this book: All Sport UK Ltd 8 (bottom, Pascal Rondeau), 10, 11, 12, 20, 22, 23, 25 (right), 34 (Tony Duffy), 36 (Steve Powell), 40 (Joe Patronite), 44; Colorsport COVER, 5, 6, 7, 8 (top), 9, 25 (left), 27, 29 (right), 30, 31, 32, 37, 38, 39, 41, 42, 43, 45; Topham Picture Library 13, 15, 16, 17, 18, 19, 24, 26, 28, 29 (left), 33, 35.

Library of Congress Cataloging-in-Publication Data

Haycock, Kate.
    Gymnastics/Kate Haycock.
       p.   cm. — (Olympic sports)
    Includes bibliographical references
    and index.
    Summary: An overview of the events that make up the gymnastics portion of the Olympic Games, with highlights of great athletes and moments.
    ISBN 0—89686—666—1
    1. Gymnastics — Juvenile literature.
    2. Olympics — History — Juvenile literature.
    3. Gymnastics.
    [1. Olympics — History]   I. Title.   II. Series.
GV461.H39   1991
796.44—dc20   91-16118

CONTENTS

OLYMPIC GYMNASTICS

When we think of the Olympic Games of today, we think of a meeting of athletes from all over the world competing in dozens of different sports. The first modern Olympics, held in Athens in 1896, was a much smaller affair: 285 athletes—all men—from just 13 countries took part in a number of sports, including track and field events and gymnastics.

In the gymnastics competition 75 participants from six countries took part. There were six events, on apparatus that were similar to those used today.

The Amsterdam Games in 1928 were the scene of the first women's gymnastics competition. This consisted of a team event with just five nations taking part. In 1952 in Helsinki, medals were awarded for exercises on individual apparatus for the first time. There were over 300 female gymnasts competing from 30 countries.

Today there are several different pieces of apparatus for both men and women in gymnastics competitions. Each gymnast needs to master all the apparatus if he or she is to succeed. It is only since 1949 that the equipment has been standardized. Before that, gymnasts would train in their home countries. On their arrival at the Olympic city, they would often find unfamiliar apparatus, with equipment of different dimensions to that on which they had always practiced their routines.

Men perform compulsory and optional exercises on six pieces of apparatus, while women perform on four. One of the most popular events with the audience is the floor exercise. This is performed by both men and women. The women, however, perform to music, while the men do not. The floor gives the gymnast a chance to demonstrate tumbling ability as well as dance skills.

Men compete in the pommel horse, the rings, the high bar, the parallel bars and the vault. Women also compete in the vault, though widthwise as opposed to the men's lengthwise. The balance beam and the uneven bars are women's events.

The format for Olympic and other national and international gymnastics competitions has changed over the years. Today, there are three phases: the team event, the all-round event—which determines the overall individual champion — and the individual apparatus. On the first day of the Olympic gymnastic competition, all competitors perform compulsory and optional exercises on all the apparatus.

▶ Li Ning raises his arms in triumph as he receives the bronze medal in the overall men's competition in Los Angeles in 1984.

Each team is represented by six gymnasts, and on each piece of apparatus the lowest score of the six is dropped. The top five scores on each of the apparatus are added together to determine the winners of the team event.

The 36 individual gymnasts with the highest combined scores from the first phase then go forward to the next phase. They compete again on each apparatus. These new scores, combined with their scores from the first phase, determine the placings for the all-round title. Current rules state that only three individuals from each competing nation may take part in these finals. The top eight scorers on each apparatus from the previous

▲ The victorious Soviet women's gymnastic team on the winner's podium in Seoul. The Soviet Union has been the dominant force in both men's and women's gymnastics for many years.

phase then participate in the final for that apparatus. Since 1984 only two gymnasts from each nation have been allowed to compete in any of these finals.

Olympic gymnastic competitions have consistently been dominated by the Eastern bloc countries: the Soviet Union and Romania, in particular. They have never failed to thrill and excite audiences, and the standards of technical and artistic excellence have constantly improved.

APPARATUS

WOMEN

The balance beam
Exquisite balance is of utmost importance in this event, which sees the majority of upsets in women's competitions. The top of the beam is only 4 in (10 cm) wide. Yet it is used to perform sophisticated movements, such as those seen in the floor exercises. Examples of these are high tumbles, walkovers and arabesques. Today many gymnasts attempt daring moves such as acrobatics and somersaults.

The uneven bars
Each bar is positioned horizontally at different heights above the floor. The gymnast performs movements that take her around each bar and from one bar to the next. Smooth flowing movements are required, and a routine usually includes moves such as twists and somersaults.

▼ May Lou Retton of the United States demonstrates a difficult move on the uneven bars. The apparatus requires tremendous strength and agility.

▲ Romanian Simona Pauca performs on the beam.

The horse vault

Men and women both perform on the vault, or horse. In women's events, it is used as a side horse, while the men use it as a long horse. It is the same apparatus turned around 90°. The women vault twice over the side horse with the highest score counting. The men have only one vault with which to try to score maximum points. The vaults performed vary in their degree of difficulty. A maximum of 10 points are decided on one short movement.

MEN

The pommel horse

The pommel horse resembles the vaulting horse with the addition of two curved wooden handles, or ''pommels,'' on the top. It dates back to medieval times when knights in armor used a similar apparatus to learn to ride or joust. Men hold the pommels with one or both hands while they swing their legs in various controlled movements and travel along the horse.

▼ The men's long horse vault.

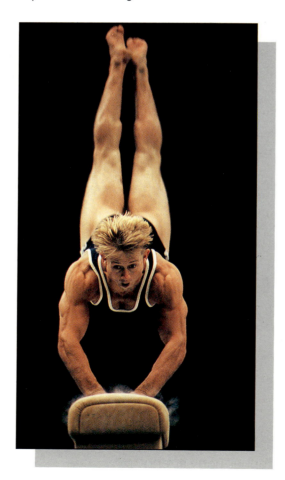

 Dmitri Bilozertchev on the rings.

It is the most unpredictable apparatus for the male competitor, relying on a fluid movement, strength (the gymnast must be able to balance his whole body on one hand) and complete concentration (only the hands may touch the horse).

The rings

The rings produce a routine with a variety of moves. They involve swinging, handstands and, most famous of all, the crucifix, where the gymnast holds his body in a straight position with his arms out to the side. The rings are suspended by wires, and only the gymnast's hands may touch the apparatus. It is an event requiring great upper-body strength.

The high bar

The high bar or horizontal bar is the most thrilling and spectacular of male events. The gymnast swings a full 360° around the bar, which is 8 ft 6 in (2.6 m) from the top of the mat, performing moves with no hands, one hand and two hands.

The parallel bars

These are two bars positioned at equal height above the floor, with a distance of 16−18 in (42−48 cm) between them. The moves can take the gymnast below and above the bars and are designed to show balance, strength and swing.

ATHENS, 1896–PARIS, 1924

In the first modern Olympics in Athens in 1896 there were six events in the men's competition: the five apparatus currently used as well as rope-climbing. The floor exercise did not appear until the next Olympics, which were held in Paris. One of the first gold medalists in the parallel bars was Alfred Flatow from Germany.

In the high bar event, only one team actually took part: Germany. Not surprisingly, the German team won the gold medal!

The 1900 Olympics in Paris are memorable only for their poor organization. As far as gymnastics was concerned, there was only one competition: the all-round title. This included 11 events—among them heaving a 110-lb stone and the pole vault, which is now a field athletics event. Although six nations were entered, all top eight positions were taken by the French—probably because they were the only people who knew what was going on!

The 1904 Olympics were held in St. Louis. The Games were something of a fiasco, lasting over a period of four and a half months. Due to the incompetence of the organizers, the host country was the only nation represented

▼ The Danish women's team put on a display in London in 1908.

▲ Sweden was the winner of the Swedish system competition in 1912.

in most of the individual events. Consequently, they won most of the medals. The team event featured 13 teams, all of which were gymnastic clubs from the United States. Today, each nation may enter only one team.

One of the most prolific medalists in 1904 — two golds, two silvers and a bronze — was American George Eyser. His feats were all the more astonishing considering he had a wooden leg! One of the more unusual events in these Games was club swinging, in which a competitor performed with two portable clubs. It was won by an American, Edward Hennig. He was very proud of the sport and won the

American championship in 1951, when he was an incredible 71 years of age.

The all-round title at the 1908 Olympics in London was won by the greatest pre-war gymnast, Alberto Braglia of Italy. In Stockholm in 1912 he became the first repeat winner of this title. Great Britain won its only individual gymnastics medal to date in 1908 with Walter Tysall's silver in the all-round event.

In the early part of the twentieth century, there were two major influences on modern gymnastics. One of these was known as the German system, which had its origins in military training and was practiced on modern apparatus. The other, the Swedish system, essentially consisted of floor-based drills, with minimal use of apparatus. Although by this time most gymnastics were based on the German system, the Swedish organizers in Stockholm introduced the Swedish system team event. Only Scandinavian teams entered, however, and the event was dropped from future Olympics.

The 1916 Games that were to be held in Berlin did not take place due to World War I. In 1920, the Belgian host city Antwerp had a very tight budget, which resulted in many events, notably individual apparatus, being withdrawn from the program. An Italian won the all-round event and also led the Italian team to victory in the team competition.

▼ The Norwegian men's team won the gymnastics "free choice" competition in Stockholm in 1912.

▲ The publicity poster for the 1924 Paris Olympic Games.

Medals for individual events returned to the Games in Paris in 1924. Rope-climbing was reintroduced, providing Czechoslovakia with its first Olympic champion, Bedrich Supcik. The side horse vault also appeared in these Games, an event now included only in women's competitions. A lawyer from Yugoslavia, Leon Stukelj, took the all-round title. He won a total of six Olympic medals in his career, including a silver in Berlin in 1936 when he was 37 years old.

Confusion arose in 1924 in the team competition. Contrary to the long-standing practice of a team of 12 men competing on each apparatus, with the top eight scores counting, the ruling was changed. Only eight men were allowed to compete, with all their scores counting. The absurdity of this was seen when a Czech team member was injured. This left the seven remaining members with the impossible task of competing against full teams. Despite performing brilliantly — four of them were placed in the top six — the team finished in last place. Fortunately, the rule was changed.

AMSTERDAM, 1928–LONDON, 1948

While women have only competed in gymnastics at the Olympic Games since 1928, and only since 1952 in individual competitions, there is no doubt that their impact has been greater in many ways that that of the men. While audiences wonder at the strength and skill of the men, the women add an element of style, emotion and elegance that has audiences flocking to the gymnastics events at every Olympics. At Los Angeles in 1984, the tickets for gymnastics competitions were sold out before any other event.

In 1928 in Amsterdam, the first women's team gold medalists were the Dutch, with Italy taking the silver and Great Britain the bronze medal.

At the same Games, 23-year-old Georges Miez of Switzerland won one silver and three gold medals. Between 1924 and 1936 Miez won a grand total of four golds, three silvers and one bronze.

The 1932 Olympics took place in Los Angeles, in the midst of the Great Depression. This, combined with the difficulty of overseas travel, affected the numbers participating and the number of events held. Standards were still high, however. The Italian team won the men's title for the fourth time in five consecutive Olympics. There were no women's events at all.

A tumbling event appeared at these Games for the first and only time. All three medals were taken by Americans, with fourth place going to the only other competitor, a Hungarian by the name of Istvan Pelle. Pelle went on to take medals in four other events, including the gold in the first individual floor event ever to be held. In previous Games, the floor event had been a team exercise, usually performed by between 16 and 45 men for a duration of up to 45 minutes. The expense of sending so many gymnasts to international competitions had finally proven too much, and the one-man floor exercise was chosen to take its place.

In the high bar event, two Finnish gymnasts tied for second place. While the judges tried to decide who should get the silver and who should get the bronze medal, the Finns discussed it among themselves. They decided that Savolainen should take the silver and Terasvirta the bronze. Today, each of the gymnasts would have received a silver medal.

The champion of the club swinging event was an American, George Roth. Roth had been unemployed for some time because of the Depression. At times he had almost starved and once went 15 days without eating.

▶ The poster for the 1936 Games in Berlin. The Games were held under the ominous gaze of Nazi leader Adolf Hitler.

BERLIN·1936
1.-16. AUG.

OLYMPISCHE SPIELE

During the Games he used to sneak food home from the Olympic village to his wife and daughter. After receiving his gold medal in front of a crowd of 60,000, he went home by the cheapest mode of transportation — hitchhiking!

The 1936 Games were held in Berlin in the ominous presence of the German leader, Adolf Hitler. The Führer intended them to be a demonstration to the world of Aryan superiority and might. They were the first Olympics to be seen on television and, although Hitler's intention failed (most notably because of the track victories of black American athlete Jesse Owens), the German leader must have been pleased by the performance of the German gymnasts. Set in the Dietrich Eckart open-air theater, which resembled a fine amphitheater, the crowd saw Konrad Frey take the gold in the parallel bars and the pommel horse. His teammate, Alfred Schwarzmann, took the gold in the long horse vault and the all-round event. The German team took the gold medal, winning by a narrow margin from the Swiss.

Eight nations competed in the women's team event, which included the uneven bars for the first time. The home nation won from the Czechs by a narrow margin.

▼ The great Finnish gymnast Heikki Savolainen takes the oath on behalf of the competitors at the opening of the Helsinki Games in 1952.

Because of their actions in World War II, the Germans and Japanese were barred from the 1948 London Olympics. The Finns, the Swiss and the Hungarians dominated the medals. In the pommel horse event, three Finns tied for first place by receiving exactly the same number of points. One of the three, Heikki Savolainen, won medals in five consecutive Olympic Games. Because of the gap of 12 years imposed by World War II, this spanned 24 years. He won his final medal, as a member of the third-placed Finnish team, in 1952 when he was 44 years old.

The gold medalist in the floor exercise, Ferenc Pataki, came from Hungary. As a child, Pataki dreamed of becoming an actor. His dream did come true, but only for a short time. His first acting part involved some acrobatic moves, which demonstrated his gymnastic talents. These were spotted and he was encouraged to take up gymnastics seriously.

The 1948 women's competition involved a degree of drama. One of the Czechoslovakian team members, 22-year-old Eliska Misakova, was taken ill shortly after her arrival in London and was confined to an iron lung. On the day of her team's appearance, she died of infantile paralysis. Misakova's elder sister competed bravely to help her team take the gold medal. At the medal ceremony, the raised Czech flag was bordered with a black ribbon.

▲ Marie Provaznikova, leader of the Czech women's team, defected in 1948.

The Games had more drama to offer: They saw the first defection by an Olympic participant. Similar incidents have taken place many times in the years since. Marie Provaznikova, the leader of the Czech women's gymnastic team, refused to return to Czechoslovakia because, she said: "There is no freedom of speech, of the press or of assembly."

One of the judges in the women's competition caused a problem in 1948 when, seemingly unaware of the maximum score of 10, she awarded a gymnast the score of 13.1!

HELSINKI, 1952–TOKYO, 1964

In 1952, in Helsinki, the whole face of Olympic gymnastics changed, as the Soviet Union sent a team for the first time in 40 years. The team's superiority must have taken the Finns, the Germans and others, who had traditionally won medals, by surprise. The Soviets won no less than five gold medals, four silver and one bronze. The winner of the all-round contest was the Soviet gymnast Viktor Chukharin. Chukharin, a Ukrainian, spent four years in a concentration camp during World War II. This horrific experience did not affect his gymnastic abilities, however, as he repeated his 1952 triumph in 1956 in Melbourne, Australia. He won a total of 11 Olympic medals.

Helsinki also featured women's individual events for the first time. The Soviet women wasted no time in demonstrating their superiority and dominated the medal positions along with the Hungarians.

One of the leading Hungarian women gymnasts in 1952 was 31-year-old Agnes Keleti, who took the gold medal in the floor exercises. She also dominated in Melbourne in 1956 where she took the gold on three out

▲ Agnes Keleti's gold-medal-winning performance on the beam in 1956.

of the four women's apparatus. In the all-round event, however, a mistake on the vault cost her the all-round title. She finished in twenty-third position. The gold medal went instead to Larissa Latynina, a Soviet girl from the Ukraine, who was 14 years her junior. In the floor exercise, they both received the same score to draw for first place.

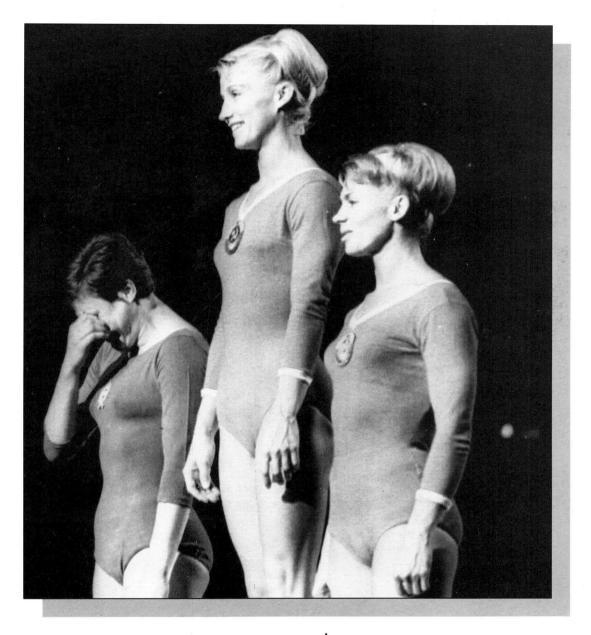

Keleti won a total of 10 Olympic medals including five golds, but after the Melbourne Games she decided not to return to Hungary and eventually settled in Israel.

The head-on contest between the Soviet Union and Hungary—in the

▲ Larissa Latynina of the Soviet Union (right) after receiving a bronze medal in the uneven bars competition.

team event, the Soviet Union beat Hungary by a very tight margin—took on deeper significance later.

A few months after the Olympics, the Hungarian government's reforms ended abruptly when Soviet tanks rolled into Budapest to crush demonstrators and to occupy the country.

The biggest challenge to the Soviet gymnasts in the men's competition came from the Japanese. The two teams vied with each other for almost every medal. In Melbourne the Soviet team took the gold medal from the Japanese in a very close contest. But in 1960 in Rome, the Japanese team triumphed. They were to hold the title for the next four Olympics, only losing it when they boycotted the Moscow Olympics in 1980.

Boris Shakhlin, another Ukrainian, was known as "The Iron Man" of gymnastics. He took baths in cold water even in the Soviet winter. He was a great master of gymnastics and won four gold medals, including the all-round title, two silvers and one bronze at the Rome Olympics. These were added to the two gold medals he had won in Melbourne four years earlier.

One of the Japanese team members, Masao Takemoto, had won a total of two silver medals and three bronze in 1952 and 1956. It took until 1960, when he was 40 years old, for him to win his first gold medal, making him the oldest gymnast in Olympic history to win a gold medal.

◀ Larissa Latynina of the Soviet Union has won more Olympic medals than any other athlete in any sport.

Larissa Latynina continued to dominate the women's competition in Rome. The Italian crowd favored the only non-East European to challenge for the medals: Keiko Ikeda, known as "Tanaka." They were so upset by the low scoring of her final routine on the uneven bars that they booed for 10 minutes until the Soviet girl, Astakhova, stepped up for her turn.

Latynina won nine gold medals during her Olympic career, as well as five silver and four bronze. She brought charm, skill and beauty to what had always been seen as a powerful masculine sport. She retired in 1964 and later became the Soviet women's coach, but not before she had vied with the new darling of gymnastics, the Czechoslovakian Vera Caslavska, for every title in the 1964 Tokyo Olympics. Caslavska succeeded in taking Latynina's all-round title from her and also defeated her on the vault.

In front of a patriotic crowd in Tokyo in 1964, the Japanese male gymnasts won the team event. Yukio Endo won the all-round title and the parallel bars, and his teammates Takuji Hayata and Haruhiro Yamashita won the rings and the long horse vault, respectively. Yamashita changed the style of vaulting and became famous for a special move on the vault: a handspring in a piked position, which became known as a "Yamashita." Indeed, the Swiss judge was so impressed that he awarded the perfect score of 10.

VERA CASLAVSKA

Czechoslovakian Vera Caslavska played a major part in popularizing women's gymnastics. Mexico City in 1968 was definitely her Olympics. Since it was also the year of the Soviet occupation of Czechoslovakia, the one-woman stand against the might of the Soviet team was all the more meaningful. The 25-year-old secretary from Prague first appeared in the Olympics in Rome in 1960 at the age of 18. She won a silver medal in the team event.

Caslavska was hugely popular with the Mexican crowd in 1968. When one of her balance beam exercises was given a score of 9.6, the audience spent 10 minutes booing and chanting, ''Ver-a, Ver-a,'' until finally her mark was increased to 9.8.

When she stepped out as the last gymnast in the floor exercises, the final event, she delighted the crowd by performing to the music of ''The Mexican Hat Dance.'' She shared first place with Larissa Petrik of the Soviet Union. This meant that the two women stood together on the top platform at the medal ceremony. They listened first to Czechoslovakia's national anthem and then to the Soviet Union's. Caslavska bowed her head and turned away, symbolizing all the sadness of her occupied country.

▼ Vera Caslavska flies onto the vault in Mexico in 1968.

▲ The extremely popular Vera Caslavska performs on the uneven bars.

The day after what turned out to be the last performance of her career, Caslavska married compatriot and 1500-m champion Josef Odlozil in a civil ceremony at the Czechoslovakian ambassador's house. When they proceeded through the streets of Mexico City to the Roman Catholic church, a crowd of 10,000 cheered them on their way.

Caslavska's style and personality made a great impact on gymnasts throughout the world. She also brought a new popularity to the sport that lasted throughout the 1960s.

In the two Olympics of 1964 and 1968 she won three and four individual golds, respectively, including the all-round championship on both occasions. She later became coach of the Czech team. As yet, no woman from that country has been able to even approach her record.

MEXICO CITY, 1968–MONTREAL, 1976

A Japanese gymnast, Akinori Nukayama, won three gold medals in Mexico in 1968 on individual apparatus. But the all-round title went to countryman Sawao Kato, who seized the gold by the narrowest margin — 0.05 of a point — from his Soviet rival Mikhail Voronin. This was also the first Olympics for Eizo Kenmotsu, one of the toughest gymnasts ever produced, who became a legend in his own lifetime. On the pommel horse, the Yugoslav Miroslav Cerar showed his supremacy by winning the gold for the second time.

◀ Miroslav Cerar of Yugoslavia demonstrates his winning form on the pommel horse in Mexico in 1968. He had also won the event in Tokyo in 1964.

killed two and held hostage nine members of the Israeli team in the Olympic village. The terrorists were allowed to go to a nearby airport, where a rescue attempt was made. All the hostages and most of the terrorists were killed. The extent of the shock and horror was unimaginable. However, the Games continued.

People's attentions were diverted from the tragedy by a young gymnast from the Soviet Union. Olga Korbut had a name that the international community could remember and pronounce and a face that many will never forget. Her bold and bewitching manner, especially in her floor routine, stole the show.

The 1972 Games in Munich produced stunning displays of gymnastic abilities. However, all sporting triumphs were overshadowed by one of the most horrific tragedies in Olympic history. Eight Arab terrorists

No one outside the Soviet Union had heard of Korbut before she came to Munich. Within a matter of days, her breathtaking performances on the beam and the floor had turned her into a worldwide sensation.

▲ The delightful Olga Korbut charms the Munich audience.

▲ The overall women's champion in 1972, the elegant Lyudmila Tourischeva.

She failed to place in the all-round competition but took the gold for the floor exercises and the beam, and took the silver on the uneven bars. The vault was not her strongest event—she finished fifth.

The gymnast who took the gold medal in the all-round event was Lyudmila Tourischeva, who displayed characteristic Soviet precision, as well as a classical elegance. But the audiences expected this from Soviet gymnasts. What they did not anticipate was the delightful personality displayed by Korbut. The fact that she could make mistakes endeared her to audiences.

In the men's competition Sawao Kato, another legendary Japanese gymnast, only 5 ft 3 in tall and weighing just 125 lbs, became the third repeat winner of the men's all-round title.

▲ The men's all-round competition at the 1972 Games in Munich saw a clean sweep for Japan. Sawao Kato (center) won the gold medal.

East Germany's first gold medal in men's gymnastics came in 1972. It was won by Klaus Koste on the long horse vault. He executed a Yamashita and a forward somersault to beat two Soviet and two Japanese gymnasts. These included the "giants," Nikolai Andrianov and Sawao Kato.

In 1976 in Montreal, the men's team competition turned into a great drama. The World Champion Shigeru Kasamatsu had been taken ill unexpectedly with appendicitis. This left the Japanese team—which included the 1968 and 1972 champion Sawao Kato, now 30 years old—under great pressure from the Soviets.

Entering the optional exercises half a point down to the Soviets, the Japanese team put on a strong performance, inspired by their determination to win their fifth consecutive Olympic team title. The tension was heightened by the judging, which was perceived by some as inconsistent and even biased. The Eastern bloc judges seemed to favor the Soviets. The audience booed loudly when Kato's rings routine was awarded 9.8 after two Soviets had previously been awarded 9.9 for what were, it was felt, weaker performances. There was a heated discussion among the judges until the President of the International Gymnastics Federation (FIG) intervened and said that Kato's score would stand.

The incredible resilience of the Japanese—in a team with an average age of 27 years—was further demonstrated by the amazing bravery of Shun Fujimoto. Fujimoto broke his leg at the knee while finishing his floor exercise routine. Not wanting to concern his coaches or fellow team members during the tense competition, Fujimoto kept the injury to himself and proceeded with his long horse vault, earning a very creditable 9.5. He then earned a 9.7 for his rings routine, but dislocated his knee on the dismount. Obviously in intense pain, which he described as feeling like "all my blood boiling in my stomach," he finally agreed to medical inspection and was persuaded to withdraw. This meant that if any Japanese team member—of the five remaining—made a mistake, the team score would suffer. They no longer had the cushion of the lowest score being dropped.

▲ Mitsuo Tsukahara was a member of the gold medal-winning Japanese men's team in Montreal in 1976.

The last event for the Soviets was the floor. Each gymnast included the most difficult moves for maximum points. The final event for the Japanese was the high bar—their strongest event. All of the first four performers put in strong routines—drawing high scores. A minor dispute over Kato's score was ignored—he held a 9.85. It all hinged on Mitsuo Tsukahara's routine. A score above 9.5 would give Japan first place; anything less would give the Soviets the gold. Despite the intense pressure, Tsukahara executed his routine superbly to score 9.9 and gave the Japanese the gold.

Tsukahara is best known for inventing a special vault move. This involves a quarter or half turn onto the horse followed by a one-and-a-half back somersault off. It has at least four variations—it can be performed straight, tucked, full-twisting or piked—and when correctly executed commands a high score.

In the pommel event a Hungarian by the name of Zoltan Magyar caused a sensation with his own innovative style. He introduced a move that became known as the "Magyar walk." It involves double leg circles one after the other. The gymnast moves from one end of the horse up and over the handles and then down to the other end of the horse without stopping. It requires a very straight body and a fast swing to ensure that the momentum is maintained.

Magyar took the gold in Montreal and in Moscow on the apparatus that he had mastered so well. Over a period of eight years he also won numerous gold medals in the event in the World and European Championships. However, he did not excel at the other events so he failed to appear in the all-round ratings.

The Soviet and East German stronghold on women's gymnastics was threatened in Montreal in 1976 by a new force—the Romanians. Their star was Nadia Comaneci, competing at the young age of 14. An incredible athlete, totally fearless of the most

▲ Zoltan Magyar of Hungary dominated the pommel horse in Montreal and in Moscow.

dangerous moves, she worked her way through routine after routine, seemingly oblivious to the millions watching her.

She astounded the world when she became the first Olympic gymnast to be awarded the combined judges' score of 10 for her performance on the balance beam and the uneven bars. She went on to receive five more 10s for her performances on various apparatus. Comaneci took golds in the all-round event, the uneven bars and the beam. It is interesting to note that this extraordinary gymnast would not have been allowed to compete if today's rules had been in place in 1976: men gymnasts must now be at least 16 years old, and women at least 15 years old.

Despite the excellence of Teodora Ungereanu, whom Nadia considered her toughest rival as well as her closest friend, Romania was unable to take the team title from the Soviet Union. The Soviet team included such names as Nelli Kim, Olga Korbut and Lyudmila Tourischeva.

The new rulings in 1976 stated that only three gymnasts from any one country could compete in the all-round finals. The absurdity of this was shown when Elvira Saadi of the Soviet Union,

an elegant performer who was a joy to watch, was eliminated from the all-round phase. She had achieved the seventh-highest individual score during the team competition. She lost out as the fourth-best Soviet competitor, while Monique Bolleboom of Holland could continue, despite ranking sixty-second out of 86. Not surprisingly, the Dutch girl finished last out of 36.

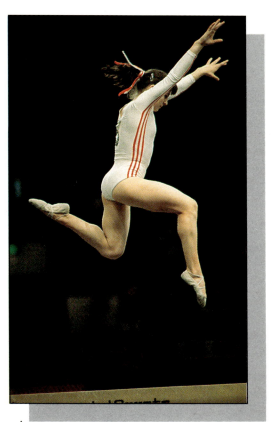

▲ Romanian Teodora Ungereanu was Comaneci's best friend and rival.

◀ Romania's Nadia Comaneci performs a perfect balance on the beam.

OLGA KORBUT

Vera Caslavska can be credited with popularizing gymnastics and will always be remembered with affection. But when Olga Korbut appeared in Munich in 1972, the effect was phenomenal. Millions of people became gymnastics fans overnight and young girls everywhere wanted to take up the sport.

The impact was even more incredible when one considers Korbut was never an all-around Olympic champion. Indeed, in Munich she finished seventh overall, behind three of her teammates. She made mistakes and her execution was often less than perfect, but that made the crowds love her even more. She had a mischievous face that captivated her audiences so that they laughed and cried with her.

Korbut was 17 when she came to Munich. She was 4 ft 11 in tall and came from a town in Byelorussia called Grodno. She had been trained and selected by a coach, Renald Knysh, who had kept a card file on young married couples in his home town whom he thought might produce future gymnasts.

Korbut qualified for the Olympic team as a substitute. She was allowed to compete only when a teammate was injured. Her spectacular routines in the team event attracted the crowd's attention immediately. She was positioned third, contributing to the victory of her team. In the all-round competition, however, disaster struck in her performance on the uneven bars. She scuffed her feet on the mat as she mounted, then slipped off the bars

▲ The impish Olga Korbut showing her usual originality and flair on the uneven bars.

during a later move and fumbled her remount. Her score was 7.5, which effectively eliminated Korbut from the running.

In the individual events, she regained her form. Winning the silver on the uneven bars behind the East German Karin Janz, she took the gold on the beam and the floor. Her daring backward somersault on the beam was a world first and her floor routine was memorable for her personality, which oozed out of it. While the champion Lyudmila Tourischeva performed with elegance and technical excellence, the audience wanted Olga. The ''Munchkin of Munich'' was a hit and she knew it.

In Montreal in 1976 she was the one the crowds came to see. Her performance did not disappoint, apart from a mishap when she fell off the beam. Audiences booed when they thought her scores too low and gave her standing ovations for her stunning routines. It came as no surprise to discover that Olga's new ambition, after her upcoming retirement from gymnastics, was to become an actress. For someone who had developed a special relationship with her audience, it seemed a fitting career.

▼ Olga Korbut, the ''Munchkin of Munich,'' was the darling of Olympic audiences because of her gymnastic brilliance and also because of her tears of disappointment.

NADIA COMANECI

A fter Munich in 1972, women's gymnastics were a huge crowd-puller thanks to Olga Korbut. In Montreal the audiences were bigger than ever before. They were there to see Korbut and the rising Soviet star, Nelli Kim, but they were also enthralled by another talent — Nadia Comaneci.

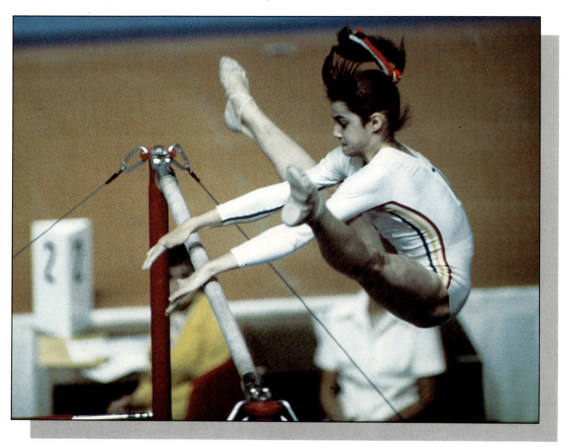

The Romanian team had been coming on in leaps and bounds under the guidance of coach Bela Karoli. In Montreal he introduced his prodigy, Nadia Comaneci, who was already the European champion. It was soon evident that this Romanian, who at 4 ft 11 in was the same height as Korbut, was gymnastics' newest phenomenon.

▲ At her first Games in Montreal, Comaneci, coached by Bela Karoli, scored the perfect 10 in the uneven bars.

In front of the 16,000 capacity crowds that packed the gymnastics arena, and on millions of television screens worldwide, she performed her first beam routine with assured confidence and great skill, almost daring the Soviets to challenge her.

Comaneci had been trained as a gymnast from the age of 6. In 1975 she had defeated Tourischeva in the European Championships and she came to Montreal, at the age of 14, the slight favorite. By the end of the team competition she had made history by being awarded the perfect 10 twice for her performances, first on the uneven bars and then on the balance beam. In the whole competition Comaneci received seven 10s while the Soviet girl, Nelli Kim, received only two.

Comaneci did not have the charisma of Korbut. Korbut had shown the world how judges, and audiences especially, like choreography and personality in the floor event. Sure enough Comaneci got the crowd clapping along with ''Yes, Sir, That's My Baby'' as she included wiggles and Charleston steps in her routine. But her real talents were her amazing daring, athleticism and her perfection. She raised the heights of gymnastics and set a new standard of perfection for which she will always be remembered.

▼ Nadia Comaneci made history at the Montreal Games by scoring seven 10s.

MOSCOW, 1980–SEOUL, 1988

he Moscow Olympics in 1980 were boycotted by a number of nations in protest over the Soviet invasion of Afghanistan. The most noticeable loss in the gymnastics arena was the Japanese team. Without its traditional rival, the Soviet men's team took the gold medal comfortably ahead of the East German team, with the biggest winning margin in post-war Olympic history.

Aleksandr Dityatin became the first person to win eight medals in one Olympic Games—three golds, four silvers and one bronze—an impressive score even despite the absence of the Japanese. He received a 10 in the long horse vault. Four more 10s were awarded in different events, including one to Zoltan Magyar for his pommel horse routine.

Soviet Nikolai Andrianov was nicknamed "Old One Leg" by some coaches who marveled at his ability to keep his legs straight and together during even the most difficult exercises. He won two golds in 1980, adding to four from 1976 and one from 1972. Four silver and three bronze brought his Olympic medal tally to an amazing 14.

The high bar champion in Moscow was the Bulgarian Stoyan Deltchev,

▼ Bulgarian Stoyan Deltchev came third in the overall competition in Moscow and first in the high bar.

▲ Davydova (left) and Comaneci shake
hands after their tremendous battle for the
overall title in Moscow.

who took the bronze in the all-round
competition. This brought his tally in
three Olympics to 12, beating the
record of Boris Shakhlin.

It was Alexander Tkatschev,
however, who created an exhilarating
move on the high bar, in a routine that
earned him 10 points during the team
event. From a swing that will pass over
the bar, the gymnast lets go of the bar
and then makes a straddle vault
backward to catch the bar once again
on the other side.

In 1980, the Soviets were again
sporting a strong women's team,
including Shaposhnikova, Filatova, Kim
and Davydova. Their superiority took
them to the gold medal, with the
ever-improving East Germans taking
the bronze. Romania's hopes of a

position higher than second were
shattered when Comaneci lost her grip
on the uneven bars and fell backward
on the floor.

In true competition style, the
contest in Moscow for the all-round
title came down to the final apparatus:
the beam. Comaneci needed a 9.95
score or higher to beat the Soviet girl
Yelena Davydova and retain her title. A
score of 9.9 would have meant that
they would have shared the gold. Since
Nadia had been awarded 9.9 and 10 on
the balance beam previously, it was
quite possible that she could beat
Davydova. The arena fell still as she

executed her routine. With her characteristic nerves of steel, she performed magnificently, with only the slightest flaw following a forward flip with a half twist.

The gymnasts and the crowd had to wait for the verdict. The judges' score was 9.85, but the Romanian head judge refused to register the score because she thought the routine deserved 9.95 points, enough to give Nadia the title. She argued for 28 minutes until she was finally ordered to register the original 9.85. Davydova, the girl whom none had named for the title, won the gold medal. Nadia shared the silver with the East German gymnast Maxi Gnauck.

Scoring controversy continued the next day during the finals for the individual apparatus. Nadia's mark for her floor exercise was suddenly upgraded to 9.95 points after 9.9 had originally appeared on the scoreboard. It was officially due to one of the judges registering the wrong score and then realizing her mistake. Rumors flew around, however, that the Romanians had successfully challenged the score, which gave Nadia a share of the title with Nelli Kim. Comaneci also revenged her loss to Davydova, beating her in the beam event.

While the American boycott of Moscow in 1980 was not badly missed in the field of gymnastics, the revenge boycott of Los Angeles in 1984 by the Soviets and most members of the Eastern bloc severely

▲ A jubilant American men's gymnastic team celebrates victory before a home crowd in Los Angeles in 1984.

affected the caliber of the contest. The absence of the pre-boycott favorite in the men's competition, the youngest-ever World Champion Dmitri Bilozertchev, was particularly noticed. Undeterred, Americans, Japanese and Chinese alike competed with gusto. On the positive side, the boycott at least gave gymnasts from other countries a chance to show their skills. In fact, in the closest men's all-round events in 60 years, 27-year-old Koji Gushiken from Japan, who placed only fifth after the preliminaries, surprised everybody and came from behind to edge Peter Vidmar of the United States into the silver position. The margin of 0.025 of a point made the Japanese emotional to the point, he said, when he felt the existence of God for the first time.

The Chinese were the new force in men's gymnastics and the reigning World Champions in the team event. Everyone was predicting a Chinese victory. The American team—three members competing in their home arena on the campus of the University of California in Los Angeles—pulled off an assured and emotional victory, leaving the Chinese the silver and the Japanese the bronze medals.

Bart Conner and Peter Vidmar were two American gymnasts who took individual gold medals, much to the delight of the ecstatic American crowd. Li Ning, from China, who was also popular with the crowd, went home from the Los Angeles Olympics with more medals than any other athlete: three gold, two silver and one bronze.

In the women's competition, the United States, Romania (who alone represented Eastern Europe) and China dominated the competition.

▼ Ecaterina Szabo of Romania performing in Los Angeles in 1984.

The team event was won by the Romanian women, starring Ecaterina Szabo, Simona Pauca and Lavinia Agache. Julianne McNamara became the first American woman to score 10 in the Olympics—in the uneven bars. Mary Lou Retton showed astounding form in the vault, scoring 10 for a Tsukahara in which she achieved unmatched height.

▼ Julianne McNamara was the first American woman to score 10 in an Olympic uneven bars competition.

The home crowd had to wait for the all-round competition to see what they had been waiting for—a United States gold medal in women's gymnastics. It was a close contest. Mary Lou Retton was fighting it out with the Romanian Szabo. With two events for each competitor remaining, Szabo led by 0.15 of a point. Retton scored 10 in the floor exercise, reducing Szabo's lead to 0.05. Hoping for 10 in her uneven bars routine, Szabo could only achieve a 9.9. Retton's nerves held and her superb vault was perfectly executed, giving her the title.

Szabo sprang back from her disappointment, however. She took gold medals in the floor exercise, the balance beam, which she shared with her teammate Simona Pauca, and the vault. She must have been particularly pleased with the latter, which she seized from Retton, in what was the American gymnast's best event. Szabo's victory on the floor was achieved after a power shortage plunged the arena into total darkness just as she was about to perform. Julianne McNamara had just completed her routine, but only when the lights were restored did Szabo see that her nearest rival had scored 10 points. To assure first place, Szabo also needed to score 10. Despite the uncertainty preceding her turn, she summoned up everything to perform perfectly, and won the gold medal 0.025 of a point ahead of McNamara. Her tally of four golds and one silver in one Olympics

▲ The superb Daniela Silivas of Romania finished second in the overall women's competition at the Seoul Games in 1988.

beat Comaneci's.

With the Eastern bloc, the United States, China and Japan in one place again for the first time since 1976, the stage was set in Seoul, South Korea, in 1988 for a truly riveting competition. The world was waiting to see the Soviet women take on the defending Olympic and World Champions: Romania.

The teams were led by Daniela Silivas for Romania and Elena Shoushounova for the Soviet Union. Each woman returned four perfect scores from the eight compulsory and optional exercises. The Soviet Union held the lead with two exercises to go when one of the team, Strazheva, injured her knee after landing awkwardly from the beam. She was carried out on a stretcher, leaving the Soviets with no margin for error. The Romanians, however, were unable to capitalize on the loss, and lost to the Soviet team.

An ever-improving American women's team was the talk of these Olympics. The team was led by Nadia Comaneci's former coach, Bela Karoli, who had defected from the East. The American team vied with the East Germans for the bronze medal in a competition that was troubled by controversy over biased scoring. The Americans were penalized for the slightest flaw despite executing more complex moves than their rivals. But the East Germans finally clinched the bronze by 0.3 of a point.

There was a Romanian and Soviet head-to-head again in the all-round competition: Silivas against Shoushounova. There was never more than 0.5 of a point in the final between the two girls. Shoushounova scored 10 on the uneven bars, and both girls were awarded 10 for their floor exercises.

The vault was the last event, as it was in the Retton-Szabo final four years before. The tension was almost

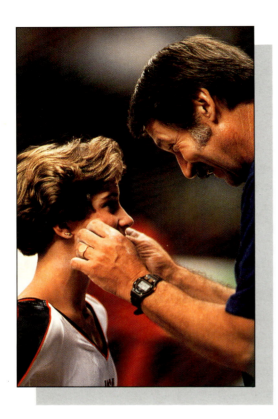

▲ Gold-medal-winning U.S. gymnast Phoebe Mills with her team coach Bela Karoli. In the 1970s and early 1980s, Karoli trained Nadia Comaneci.

unbearable as Silivas stepped up to take her vault. Her score was 9.95. Shoushounova needed 9.975 to tie and 10 to win. With her first vault, the Soviet made a faultless execution. She earned her 10 with one vault to spare and, with it, the gold medal. Romanians and Soviets vied for the next four places, proving their unrivaled superiority in women's gymnastics.

In Los Angeles, Szabo had taken a hat-trick of gold medals after losing the all-round title. Her teammate, Daniela Silivas, now earned similar awards. Silivas took three golds and a bronze on the vault, while Shoushounova skidded during her floor routine and could manage only one silver and one bronze.

There was delight in the American camp when Phoebe Mills won the first medal in 40 years for an American woman in a non-boycotted Games. Women's gymnastics in the United States were finally on the map.

Soviet dominance in men's gymnastics returned with a vengeance to Seoul in 1988. The last time the Soviets had won an Olympic team competition without a major boycott was 32 years earlier in Melbourne. The Soviet athletes were determined to reassert their superiority: They dominated every piece of apparatus and took the team gold with ease. The Americans could not muster the form of 1984, and the East Germans took the silver from the Japanese, with the Chinese and the Bulgarians close behind.

The supremacy of the Soviet gymnasts gave their country all three medals in the all-round competition. The gold went to Vladimir Artemov, after a close contest with Dmitri Bilozertchev, who had nearly lost his leg in a car accident three years earlier. Valeri Lioukina took the bronze. The new rules allowed only three members from one team to compete in the all-round event. The Soviet team was so strong that any of the six members could easily have dominated the individual event. Bilozertchev recorded the highest-ever score in an Olympic final — 59.75 — dropping only 0.25 point in all six events. However, he did not carry forward enough points to win.

It was no surprise to anyone after the dominance of the Soviet gymnasts in the competition so far that they took six golds, although in total 11 golds were presented. The pommel horse had a triple tie — Bilozertchev, the Hungarian and Borkai and Gueraskov from Bulgaria, all of whom scored 10. As Zsorlt Borkai said: "The difference between us is too small for the human mind to distinguish."

▼ Vladimir Artemov won the men's overall gold medal in Seoul in 1988.

An emotional moment for the Korean crowd was the country's first medal in gymnastics — a bronze in the vault awarded to Jong-Hoon Park, who only just qualified for the final. He rose to the occasion, however, and his first vault earned a 9.95. His second vault was better than his first, and the arena exploded when the judges flashed up the figure 10.

In Olympic history, the dominant nations in men's gymnastics have included Italy, Switzerland, Finland, Japan and now, overwhelmingly, the Soviet Union. But the Olympics have always been full of surprises and, with nations such as China, the United States and Germany developing ever stronger teams, who can predict the future champions?

ALEKSANDR DITYATIN

Brought to gymnastics school at the age of 8, Aleksandr Dityatin was awkward and round-shouldered—certainly not a gymnastics "natural."

The gymnastics world first heard the name of Aleksandr Dityatin in 1972 when he became junior champion of the Soviet Union, but his growing body was making it difficult

for him to perform the more complex moves. Through his own perseverance and that of his coach, however, he was able to use his size—5 ft 10 in. He managed to achieve a wider range of movements and greater height than many of his closest rivals.

He took his first Olympic medal in Montreal in 1976—a silver in the rings —but missed months of competition shortly after that due to a serious leg injury. Determined, he worked hard to return to Olympic gymnastics in Moscow in 1980, where his amazing consistency impressed gymnasts and commentators alike. He became the first person to win eight medals in one Olympic competition.

► Dityatin was the master of the rings, the apparatus that is considered by many people to be the most difficult. Swinging back and forth from the handstands calls for an incredibly strong back and shoulders. The held positions, such as this demonstrated by the Soviet gymnast, also require enormous strength, especially in the arms and shoulders. Dityatin won his first Olympic medal for the rings—a silver in Montreal.

◄ Soviet gymnast Aleksandr Dityatin performs his gold medal-winning floor routine at the 1980 Moscow Games before an appreciative home audience.

RHYTHMIC GYMNASTICS

Rhythmic gymnastics became an Olympic event in 1984 in Los Angeles. It is a branch of gymnastics that has been increasing in popularity for some years and is seen as a contrast to the gymnastics performed on fixed apparatus, highlighting as it does the more artistic qualities.

In rhythmic gymnastics, the gymnasts perform a series of routines, one with each of a range of small hand apparatus. These are selected from the ball, the hoop, the ribbon, clubs and the rope. Each routine is performed on a carpeted area of 39 ft² (12 m²) and is worked to music.

Currently, only women perform in this branch of gymnastics. The movements require suppleness, co-ordination, control of the apparatus and poise. The idea is that the piece of apparatus being used appears to be part of the body's movements.

In the Olympics there is currently only one rhythmic gymnastics event — the all-round title. The competition has two phases. In the preliminary rounds all the gymnasts — of which no more than two may be from any one country — perform with each of the four selected apparatus. The top 20 go forward to the finals when they again perform four routines to decide the overall champion.

The apparatus used in 1984 were the hoop, the ball, the ribbon and clubs.

▶ Lori Fung of Canada won the first Olympic gold medal for rhythmic gymnastics in Los Angeles in 1984.

Thirty-three gymnasts took part, representing 20 nations.

The winner in the first competition in 1984 surprised everybody. The Canadian Lori Fung, who had finished twenty-third in the 1983 World Championships, beat the favorite, Romanian Doina Staiculescu, for the gold medal. Ironically, they had spent a month training together in Romania.

INDEX

The numbers in **bold** refer to captions.